Paige
the Christmas
Play Fairy

For Zoë Sarankin, a very good
friend of the fairies
Special thanks to
Narinder Dhami

ISBN 978-0-545-22177-1

12 11 10 9 8 7 6 5 4 3   11 12 13 14 15/0

Printed in the U.S.A. 40

First Scholastic Printing, September 2010

Paige
the Christmas
Play Fairy

by Daisy Meadows

SCHOLASTIC INC.

New York   Toronto   London   Auckland

Sydney   Mexico City   New Delhi   Hong Kong

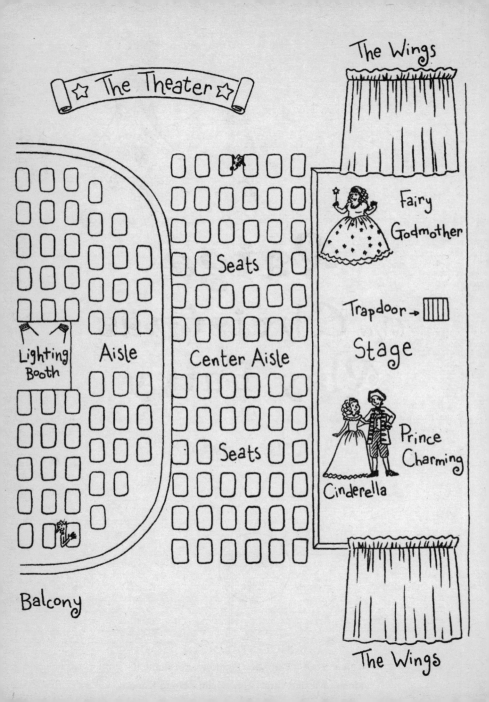

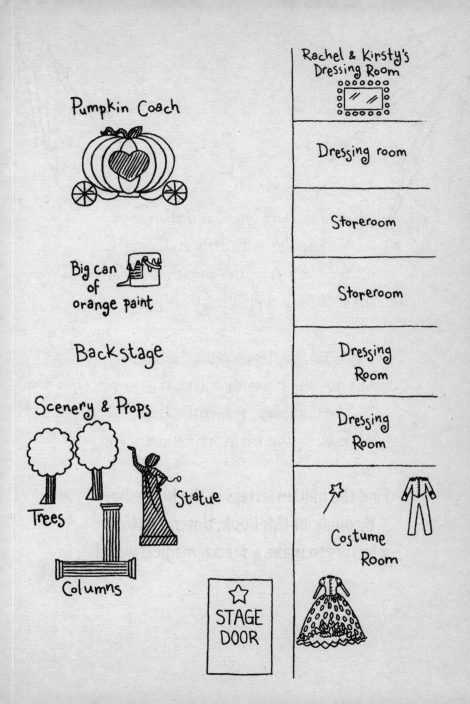

Pumpkin Coach

Big can of orange paint

Backstage

Scenery & Props

Trees

Columns

Statue

STAGE DOOR

Rachel & Kirsty's Dressing Room

Dressing room

Storeroom

Storeroom

Dressing Room

Dressing Room

Costume Room

Christmas plays (more fun than toys)
Are popular with girls and boys,
But now this year, this month, this day,
I will spoil their Christmas plays.

Goblins, go, leave right this hour!
Bring me the items that have the power
To ruin plays across the land,
And destroy the fairies' Christmas plans!

Find the hidden letters in the horseshoes throughout this book. Unscramble all 7 letters to make a special magical word!

Ballet slipper
Slip-up

Contents

Casting Crisis

"Only three more days until Christmas!" Rachel Walker said, skipping down High Street in Tippington and beaming happily at her best friend, Kirsty Tate. "I'm so glad you could come visit, Kirsty, even if it's just for a few days."

"Me, too," Kirsty agreed, looking excited. She had arrived the day before, and her parents were coming to Tippington again to pick her up on Christmas Eve. "I hope it snows, don't you? It makes Christmas so magical."

"And magic is something we know all about!" Rachel exclaimed, laughing. Kirsty knew exactly what Rachel meant. Ever since the two girls had met on a magical vacation to Rainspell Island, they had become best friends with the fairies!

"One, two, three!" Rachel counted as she practiced her dance steps along the sidewalk. "This is the trickiest step in my dance for the Christmas play. I want it to be perfect."

Rachel was dancing in the Tippington Christmas play. It was always a big production of a well-known show. This year, they were doing a performance of Cinderella. On Christmas Eve, Rachel would be one of four girls dancing in the big ballroom scene. Rachel and Kirsty were on their way to Tippington Theater, for a rehearsal.

"Thanks for inviting me to the rehearsal," Kirsty said as they reached the theater. "I wish I could come to the actual performance."

"Me, too," Rachel agreed, looking glum. "But the show is always so popular that the tickets sold out really fast. I couldn't even get any for my mom and dad!" Then she brightened. "We're practicing the ballroom scene today, though, so at least you'll get to see my dance." The girls went in through the stage door. There was a lot of hustle and bustle backstage, and Kirsty looked around with interest.

"Rachel! Kirsty!" a girl's voice called.

The girls turned and saw Karen Lewis, a friend of Rachel's from school, waving at them and looking really excited.

"Karen is one of the dancers in the ballroom scene, too," Rachel told Kirsty, as Karen came rushing over.

"Rachel, our costumes are here!" Karen said with a big smile.

"Oh!" Rachel looked thrilled. "I thought they weren't coming until the final rehearsal tomorrow."

"Well, they're here now!" Karen laughed. "I can't wait to see what we're wearing."

The three girls hurried to the room backstage where the costumes had been laid out. Most of the cast members were there already. There was a buzz of excited chatter!

Rachel glanced around the room at the colorful costumes, which all had labels pinned to them.

"Ours are over here!" Karen called

from the other side of the room.

Rachel and Kirsty hurried to look. A beautiful white ballet dress with puffy white layers lay on a chair. It was labeled RACHEL. Next to the dress was a pair of pink satin ballet shoes with long ribbons, and a pink rose for Rachel to wear in her hair. All four dancers had the same costume.

"Oh, it's beautiful!" Kirsty breathed.

"I can't wait to try it on," said Rachel, holding the dress out in front of her.

Just then, a short man carrying a clipboard came into the room. He looked very worried. "Karen, Rachel, please go and change into your costumes right away," he said, patting his forehead with a spotted handkerchief. "I'm afraid we have all sorts of problems. Nobody's costume fits properly, and the seamstress doesn't think she's going to have time to alter them

8

all. We need to know if your costumes fit you."

"Yes, Mr. Robinson," said Rachel. Kirsty remembered Rachel telling her that he was the director of the show.

"Mr. Robinson!" a stagehand cried, rushing into the room. "Clarissa Murray's mom just called. Clarissa has the chicken pox. She can't dance in the show!"

"What?" Mr. Robinson groaned. "Oh, no!"

"How terrible!" Kirsty said. "Poor Clarissa."

Mr. Robinson was pacing anxiously back and forth. "The dance won't work with just three girls," he muttered. "We need four. Oh, this is a disaster!"

Kirsty and Rachel glanced at each other. Kirsty knew that they were both thinking the same thing.

"Maybe I could take Clarissa's place!" Kirsty suggested breathlessly.

Paige Appears

Mr. Robinson turned in surprise. "And who are you, my dear?" he asked.

"Kirsty Tate," replied Kirsty. "I'm Rachel's friend, and I'm staying with her until Christmas Eve."

"I can teach Kirsty the steps," Rachel added quickly.

"And I'll practice every single minute

until the show!" said Kirsty.

"Well, that solves our problem!" Mr.
Robinson said,
looking delighted.
"Thank you so
much!" He
glanced at
Kirsty. "You
look about the
same size as Clarissa.
Why don't you try
on her costume and see if it fits?"
Then he hurried off.

"Isn't this great?" Rachel said with a
big smile. "Now you're going to be in
the show, too!"

Kirsty grinned. "I just hope I can learn
the steps in time," she said.

They found the dress labeled CLARISSA and Kirsty picked it up. The rose for her hair was there, too, but there was only one pink ballet shoe.

"Rachel, one of the shoes is missing," she said with a frown.

"It must be somewhere around here," Rachel replied. "Let's look for it."

The girls searched the room, but the ballet shoe was nowhere to be found. They went to tell Mr. Robinson about the problem.

"The costumes were stored in the small dressing room at the end of the hall," he said, pointing it out. "The shoe probably got left behind in there. Actually . . ." he

DRESSING
ROOM 2

went on, thoughtfully, "no one's using that dressing room. Why don't you girls take it? Then you'll have some space to practice the dance."

Rachel and Kirsty glanced at each other in delight. "Thank you!" they said together. They hurried down the hallway, carrying their costumes.

When Kirsty opened the door of the dressing room, it was dark inside. Rachel flicked on the light switch. Instantly, a mirror surrounded by light bulbs filled the room with a dazzling white light.

A second later, one of the bulbs popped loudly and went out. The noise made Rachel and Kirsty jump.

"Rachel, look!" Kirsty gasped.

Sparkling gold fairy dust had burst from the broken bulb. As the dust cleared, Rachel and Kirsty saw a pretty little fairy dancing in the air in front of them!

"Hello," the fairy called. "I'm Paige the Christmas Play Fairy!"

"Hi, Paige," the girls replied. The tiny fairy wore a short red ballet dress sparkling with diamond dust, a starry headband, and red ballet shoes with tiny bows.

Quickly, Rachel closed the dressing room door. Meanwhile, Paige pointed her wand at the broken bulb. A second later, it was shining as brightly as the others again.

"I'm so glad to see you, girls!" Paige cried. "It's my job to make sure that all the Christmas plays are fun and exciting,

so that everyone has a merry
Christmas." She crossed her arms
and looked very determined. "But I
need your help. Jack Frost is up to his
old tricks again!" she went on, frowning.
"He wants to ruin Christmas—for
everybody!"

Christmas Play Problem

Kirsty and Rachel gasped.

"But why?" Rachel asked.

"Because he didn't get the part he wanted in the Fairyland Christmas Play!" Paige replied, landing lightly on Rachel's shoulder. "Jack Frost wanted to be Prince Charming. Instead, he got the part of Second Tree in the forest scene."

"What did he do?" Rachel asked anxiously.

Paige looked glum. "There are three special magic shoes, which help me do my job," she explained. "Jack Frost sent his goblins to steal them! If they do, all the magic that makes the Christmas plays special will vanish!"

"What do the magic shoes look like?" Kirsty asked.

"One is a ballet shoe," Paige replied. "It makes sure that all the costumes fit properly.  The second is a horseshoe, which makes the props work and ensures that the scene changes go 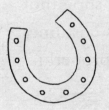 smoothly. And the last one is Cinderella's glass slipper. That helps everyone remember their lines."

Kirsty and Rachel looked at each other with wide eyes.

"So our show might be a disaster because of Jack Frost!" cried Rachel with dismay.

Paige nodded and flew over to Kirsty.

"One of your ballet shoes is missing, right?" she asked.

Kirsty nodded. "That's because it's not just any old shoe," Paige went on. "It's the magic shoe that makes everyone's costumes fit properly."

"Mr. Robinson told us that nobody's outfits were the right size," Rachel said. "That must be because the magic ballet shoe is missing!"

"I have to find that shoe," Paige said, biting her lip anxiously.

"Otherwise, all the boys and girls who go to see Christmas plays will be so disappointed!"

"We'll help you, Paige," Rachel promised.

Kirsty nodded. "Of course we will," she agreed.

Paige smiled and twirled up into the air, skirt flying. "Thank you, girls!" she cried. "I knew you wouldn't let me down!"

"Where should we start?"asked Kirsty.

But before Rachel or Paige could

reply, the dressing room door opened
very slowly. Paige zoomed to hide
behind Rachel's shoulder.

A moment later, the knobbly green
head of a goblin appeared around the

door! Rachel and Kirsty held their breaths. But they could hardly believe their eyes when they saw what the goblin had clutched in his hand—a pink ballet shoe!

Get that Goblin!

The goblin was obviously looking for a place to hide—so he jumped when he saw Rachel and Kirsty! Scowling, he hid the ballet shoe clumsily behind his back. Then he left the room, slamming the door and running off down the hallway.

"That goblin had my magic ballet slipper!" Paige gasped. "After him!"

The girls flung the door open and ran after the goblin. Paige clung to Rachel's shoulder. They followed the sound of running footsteps into the area behind the stage. The stagehands were getting the props ready for rehearsal. Luckily, they were too busy to notice the girls!

"Where did the goblin go?" Kirsty wondered out loud.

"There are three different ways he could have gone," Rachel said anxiously. "How will we find him now?"

"He must be here somewhere," Paige whispered in Rachel's ear.

Just then, two stagehands walked by, carrying a marble column for the ballroom scene.

"I didn't think there were any goblins in Cinderella, did you?" one of the stagehands said to the other.

"No," his friend agreed, "but that was really a great costume. It was so ugly!"

Rachel and Kirsty glanced at each other. "They saw the goblin!" Rachel whispered. "And they came from over there," Kirsty added, pointing.

The girls dashed toward where the stagehands had been. Soon, they came to an area where big props from previous plays were stored. It was dark and shadowy, but the girls could make out statues, trees, bushes, and big cans of paint, plus doors, tables, chairs, and other pieces of furniture.

"The goblin could be hiding in here anywhere," Paige said, fluttering around to examine the props. "We'll have to keep our eyes open."

Rachel and Kirsty began to search for the goblin. They looked behind trees and statues, and under tables and chairs, but he was nowhere to be seen.

"What next?" Kirsty asked gloomily.

Rachel was just about to reply when she caught a glimpse of something out of the corner of her eye. She spun around to look at a group of statues. As she watched, one of them moved!

Rachel nudged Kirsty. "That statue

moved!" she whispered, pointing at it.

"And it has a really long nose," Kirsty whispered back. "I bet it's the goblin!"

As the girls and Paige began to creep toward him, the goblin realized

he'd been spotted. With a shriek, he ran
to the back of the prop area.

The girls ran after him. They saw the
goblin head for the ladder that led to
the catwalk high overhead. The goblin
clamped the ballet slipper between his
teeth and began climbing.

Rachel, Kirsty, and Paige
hurried over to the
bottom of the
ladder.

"Come down!"
called Paige.

The goblin
glared at her,
but kept climbing.
The girls and
Paige watched as
he went higher
and higher. Suddenly,
he began to slow
down. The girls saw him
glance at the floor nervously.
A look of panic came over
his face and he clutched the
sides of the ladder. He looked

scared that he was going to fall! "I think the goblin just realized that he's afraid of heights!" Rachel whispered. "Why don't you come down?" Paige called up to him. The goblin shook his head stubbornly. Taking a deep breath, he closed his eyes and continued climbing. "With his eyes closed, he won't

be able to see where he's going!" Kirsty
exclaimed.

Suddenly, the goblin missed a rung
of the ladder—and his foot slipped!
He gave a frightened yell. The ballet
shoe fell from his mouth. As it whirled
downward, ribbons flying, the goblin

reached out to grab it. He missed,
and he also lost his grip on the ladder.

As Rachel darted forward and caught
the ballet shoe, the goblin fell. He
tumbled through the air, arms flailing
wildly — and he looked terrified!

It's Raining Goblins!

"Oh, no!" Kirsty cried. "We have to break his fall!" She glanced around and spotted a big can of orange paint next to Cinderella's pumpkin coach.

"Paige!" Kirsty yelled, pointing at the can of paint.

Luckily, Paige understood exactly what

Kirsty meant. She waved her wand.
A shower of magical golden sparkles
swirled around the can, pushing it across
the floor until it was right underneath
the goblin.

SPLASH!

The goblin plunged into the can!

Orange paint drops splattered
everywhere. The goblin surfaced,
spluttering and wiping
orange streaks from his
face. "Give me that
ballet shoe!" he
gurgled angrily,
climbing out
of the can.

"No way!" Rachel
replied firmly, hiding
the shoe behind her
back. "It's not
yours."

"Go back to Fairyland," said
Kirsty. "And tell Jack Frost we're
not going to let him ruin
Christmas!"

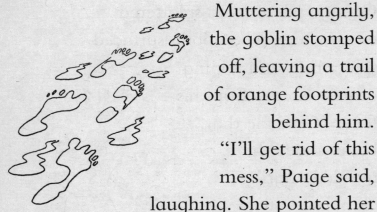

Muttering angrily, the goblin stomped off, leaving a trail of orange footprints behind him. "I'll get rid of this mess," Paige said, laughing. She pointed her wand at the footprints. Soon, all the orange paint had vanished in a stream of sparkles.

"Thank goodness we have the magic ballet shoe back," Paige went on happily, flying over to perch on Kirsty's shoulder. "Now

your costumes will fit properly, and so
will everyone else's."

"We'd better go
and see Mrs.
Spencer, the
seamstress, Kirsty,"
Rachel suggested.
"Then the ballet
shoe's magic
can get to work.
Plus, she'll be so
happy that she
doesn't have to alter everyone's costumes
after all!"

Rachel led the way to the costume
department, where she, Kirsty, and
Paige peeked into the room. It was
full of actors and actresses, all dressed

in their costumes. Mrs. Spencer, the seamstress, was rushing here and there with a tape measure around her neck and a box of pins in her hand.

"Mrs. Spencer!" Karen Lewis cried, twirling in circles. Her white dress swirled around her. "Look, I don't think my

dress is too long after all. In fact, it's just right!"

"And I can button my jacket now!" added the young man who was playing Prince Charming. "It felt too small a minute ago."

"Oh, thank goodness!" Mrs. Spencer

sighed with relief.
"It looks like we
all panicked too
soon."

Paige beamed at
the girls. "The ballet
shoe's magic is working again!" she
announced joyfully.

"Let's go and change, too, Kirsty,"
said Rachel.

Kirsty and Rachel hurried back to

their dressing room
with Paige close
behind. Quickly,
they changed into
their beautiful
dresses, which
fit perfectly.

Then Paige helped put the roses in their hair.

"You look so pretty!" Paige said.

Rachel and Kirsty grinned happily at each other.

"I need to get back to Fairyland and tell everyone the good news," Paige went on. "Good luck with your rehearsal, girls. I'll see you tomorrow. But don't forget, the goblins will definitely be back to cause more trouble! So keep an eye out." With a flick of her wand, she vanished in a cloud of dazzling fairy dust.

"Kirsty, we'd better start practicing the dance steps," Rachel said. "There's a lot to learn before the play."

"And we only have two days before opening night!" Kirsty said eagerly. "I don't want to make any mistakes. I want the play to be really good!"

"I'm sure it will be," Rachel said. "But we'll also have to stop the goblins from stealing the magic horseshoe and the glass slipper. We *can't* let Jack Frost ruin our Christmas play!"

More Missing Magic

Contents

The Christmas Play Ponies

The next morning, the girls arrived at the theater bright and early, ready for the final dress rehearsal. Kirsty and Rachel had been very busy practicing their dance whenever they had a moment.

"We practiced so much, I think I was dancing in my sleep last night!" Kirsty laughed. "I don't want to make any mistakes today."

"Everyone thought you did great yesterday," Rachel said. "I mean, we only had about half an hour to practice in our dressing room before we went on stage!"

"Yes, but today we're going to be doing the whole show from beginning to end," Kirsty reminded her. "That means the whole cast will be there, so I want to do it right."

"I can't wait to see Cinderella's pumpkin coach," Rachel said, as they went through the stage door.

"Alison, the actress who plays the Fairy Godmother, owns a riding stable. She's bringing two ponies to pull the coach onto the stage!"

"Oh!" Kirsty exclaimed. "Do you think one of the ponies will be wearing Paige's magic horseshoe?"

Rachel nodded. "I hope so," she answered. "But we'll have to watch out for goblins! If they steal the horseshoe, none of the props will work. And who knows what could happen with the scenery?"

"We have to stop them," replied Kirsty. "Or Jack Frost will ruin all the Christmas plays everywhere!"

As the girls headed to their dressing

room, they noticed a crowd of people standing in the wings of the stage. The people were gathered around two beautiful white ponies, which were harnessed to a dazzling orange-and-gold pumpkin coach.

"Look!" Rachel gasped. "The ponies are here."

"Let's go and see," Kirsty said eagerly. The girls hurried over to join the admiring crowd. The ponies had been carefully groomed, and their white coats gleamed. They wore pretty golden halters and glittering golden headdresses with fluffy orange feathers.

"Aren't they beautiful?" Rachel said, stroking the pony closest to her. Both animals were very well-behaved and stood patiently as people pet them.

"They even have golden horseshoes!" whispered Kirsty, pointing down at the ponies' sparkling hooves. "I wonder which is the magic one." The girls tried to look closer at the ponies' horseshoes, but it was hard to do with so many other people around.

"Isn't the pumpkin coach fantastic, too?" Rachel said. "This is going to be the best part of the whole show!"

Suddenly the director
hurried over, clutching
his clipboard. "Time
for you all to get
changed for the
dress rehearsal,"
he called. "The
ponies are going
to practice pulling
the coach on and

off the stage a few times before we start,
so we need to clear some space."

Rachel and Kirsty gave the ponies one
last pat and dashed off to their dressing
room.

"I wonder if Paige will be waiting for
us," Kirsty said as they went inside.

But there was no sign of the little fairy. Quickly, the girls changed into their dresses and ballet shoes, and put the flowers in their hair.

"We'd better go to the makeup room now," Rachel said, once they both had their costumes on.

When the two girls were ready, it was

time for the dress rehearsal to begin. Kirsty and Rachel hurried to join the rest of the cast.

"I'm really nervous," Kirsty said. "I hope I can remember everything!"

"You were wonderful yesterday, Kirsty," said Lucy, the fourth dancer in the group. "You hardly made a single mistake."

"You'll be great today, too!" Rachel told her friend confidently.

Everyone was milling around backstage, dressed in their costumes.

Rachel and Kirsty were thrilled to see Cinderella in her rags; the ugly stepsisters in their tall wigs and huge dresses; and a very handsome Prince Charming.

"Attention, everyone!" Mr. Robinson said as he bustled in. "Cinderella and the ugly stepsisters on stage for the first scene, please. Everyone else can wait here until they're called." He turned

to Rachel and Kirsty. "Could you two help out by carrying the ugly stepsisters' trains, please?"

Rachel and Kirsty laughed as the ugly stepsisters headed toward the stage. They wore big puffy dresses—one striped purple and yellow, the other bright pink with purple spots. Both dresses had long, dragging trains.

Rachel and Kirsty picked up the ugly stepsisters' trailing skirts and helped them take their places in the wings. Then the girls found a quiet spot where they could watch without getting in anyone's way. There was a burst of music, and the dress rehearsal began.

The girls enjoyed themselves as they watched the familiar story unfolding before them. They felt sorry for Cinderella when the ugly stepsisters wouldn't let her go to the ball, and they wanted to cheer when the Fairy Godmother arrived in Cinderella's kitchen.

"You *will* go to the ball, Cinderella!" declared the Fairy Godmother. "Bring me a pumpkin!"

Rachel nudged Kirsty and pointed at the wings on the opposite side of the stage. The ponies were ready to pull the pumpkin coach on stage. As the Fairy Godmother waved her wand over the ordinary pumpkin that Cinderella brought her, there was a glittering flash of smoke. A stagehand quickly removed the pumpkin. At the same moment, another stagehand sent the ponies trotting onto the stage. The coach glittered and the ponies' white coats gleamed in the bright spotlights.

Kirsty and Rachel couldn't help gasping.

"Isn't it cool, the way the pumpkin disappears and the coach takes its place?" Kirsty whispered. "It's just like real magic!"

Rachel nodded. "The audience is going to love it!" she whispered.

Suddenly, a piece of wooden scenery that was painted to look like a kitchen cabinet full of shelves of plates toppled over. It fell to the floor with a loud *BANG!* Everyone jumped, and the ponies were startled, too. They whinnied with fright and broke into a

canter, dashing across the stage past
Cinderella and the Fairy Godmother,
and dragging the coach behind them.

"The ponies are really scared, Kirsty,"
Rachel cried. "We have to stop them!"

Pony Problems

The ponies galloped into the wings
where Rachel and Kirsty were standing.
The two girls quickly stepped forward
and grabbed the ponies' golden lead
ropes, bringing them safely to a stop.

"That wasn't supposed to happen!"
they heard Mr. Robinson wail from the
front row of the theater.

"It's OK," Rachel said soothingly, patting the pony closest to her on the nose. "Calm down." As she stroked the pony, she noticed one extra-bright sparkle in the middle of its feathered headdress. Suddenly, Paige popped out from between the orange feathers.

"Hello, girls!" she whispered. As Rachel heard footsteps running across the stage toward them, Paige fluttered to hide on Kirsty's shoulder.

Alison, the ponies' owner, dashed over to Kirsty and Rachel, holding up the long skirt of her Fairy Godmother costume. "Oh, you managed to catch them!" she said gratefully. "Thanks, girls. I should have stopped them myself, but I wasn't expecting them to bolt like that!"

"I think they're fine now," Kirsty replied, handing the lead ropes to Alison.

"I'll just check them out," Alison said, running her hand up and down the ponies' legs. "Oh, no!" she exclaimed suddenly. "Snowflake lost one of her shoes!"

Kirsty and Rachel could see that the golden horseshoe on Snowflake's front left hoof was missing.

"I don't understand it," Alison went on, shaking her head. "Both horses had all four of their shoes before the dress rehearsal!"

"Maybe Snowflake lost her shoe on the stage," Rachel suggested.

"Or in the wings," Kirsty added.

Alison nodded. "If I can find it, my blacksmith will be able to fit it for the performance," she said, and hurried off.

The next moment, Paige peeked out from under Kirsty's hair. "Girls, the missing horseshoe is no ordinary shoe," she announced. "It's the magic horseshoe!"

Kirsty and Rachel looked at each other.

"So that's why the piece of scenery fell over!" exclaimed Rachel. "It's because the magic horseshoe is missing!"

Paige nodded. "I think the goblins used some of Jack Frost's magic to make the horseshoe fall off," she explained. "Girls, we *must* get the horseshoe back—and fast!"

Horseshoe Hunting

"So there are goblins around somewhere," said Rachel, glancing over her shoulder. "We'd better keep our eyes open."

Just then, Mr. Robinson called everyone onto the stage.

"We need to find the golden horseshoe as quickly as possible," he declared.

"Otherwise, Snowflake can't perform in the play. Can someone please go get the rest of the cast so that everyone can help look?"

Rachel and Kirsty began searching for the horseshoe around the wings. Suddenly, Rachel jumped as she heard a door slam at the back of the auditorium, near the theater's lobby. Rachel frowned. Why would anyone leave the auditorium to search the lobby? The ponies hadn't been brought in through the main entrance.

Rachel nudged Kirsty. "I think

that was a goblin going into the lobby,"
she whispered.

"Let's go and see," Paige said eagerly.

The girls left the stage and hurried up
the aisle. No one noticed—they were
all too busy looking for the horseshoe!
Rachel pulled the
heavy door open
and the two girls
slipped into the lobby.

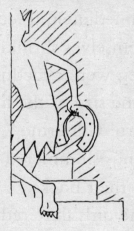

"Look!" Kirsty cried,
pointing at the stairs
leading up to the
balcony seats. A goblin
was just disappearing around
the curve in the stairs. In his hand
was a gleaming, glittering, golden
horseshoe.

"We have to catch him, girls!" Paige called. "Let me turn you into fairies. We'll be quicker that way."

Rachel and Kirsty stood still as Paige showered them with fairy magic. Immediately, they found themselves shrinking until they were exactly the same size as the little fairy! Glittering wings shimmered on their backs. The girls fluttered into the air and followed Paige up the balcony staircase.

"I can't see the goblin," Rachel said anxiously as they reached the top of the stairs.

"He could be hiding in the rows of seats," Kirsty pointed out. Paige and the girls flew slowly above the seats, searching for the goblin. Suddenly, Rachel spotted him. "There he is!" she whispered, pointing. On the right side of the balcony, a goblin's head was poking up from behind a row of seats. The friends flew over and hovered high

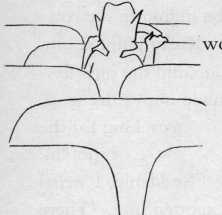

above him so he wouldn't notice them. They could see both of his hands, and it was clear that he didn't have the horseshoe.

"He must have hidden it somewhere," Paige declared.

"But look over there," Kirsty said pointing at the back row of seats on the left side of the balcony. "There's another goblin!"

Sure enough, another green head was peeking over the seats. Paige, Kirsty, and Rachel rushed over, but to their dismay, that goblin didn't have the horseshoe, either.

"Oh, no!" Paige sighed. "How many goblins *are* there?"

"And which one has the horseshoe?" Rachel added.

The girls had to figure out what to do next—and fast!

Goblin Behind the Glass

"Let's split up and each search a section of the balcony," Kirsty suggested.

"Good idea," Paige agreed.

Rachel flew over to the right side of the balcony, Kirsty to the left, and Paige took the middle. Kirsty flew along the rows, but she couldn't see any other goblins. Just then, Kirsty caught sight of

a burst of golden sparkles
coming from Paige's
wand in the middle
of the center row of
seats. Paige was doing
a little dance in the air,
and pointing down. *Paige
found the magic horseshoe!* Kirsty realized
with excitement.

Rachel had noticed, too. Both girls
zoomed over to Paige, who could hardly
contain her excitement. Her cheeks
rosy, she pointed her wand at a goblin
crouched in the middle row. There, in
his knobbly green hand,
the magic golden
horseshoe glittered!
But at that
moment, the goblin

glanced up. He gave a loud yelp
when he saw Paige and the girls and
immediately scrambled
away. He ran to the
end of the row, then
dashed up the aisle and
into a small booth
at the back of the
balcony.

"Where's he going?" Kirsty asked as
they flew after him.

"That's the sound and lighting booth,"
Rachel explained. "It's where the
engineer controls all the microphones
and spotlights and special effects for the
play."

The goblin had slammed the door of
the booth shut behind him, so the girls
flew to the front and looked in

through the window. Hovering at the glass, Paige and the girls could see that the goblin had used a chair to wedge the door shut.

"There's no way we can get in, not even if Paige makes us human-size again!" Kirsty pointed out. "How are we going to get the horseshoe now?"

The goblin inside the booth looked very pleased with himself. "Nah, nah!" He stuck out his tongue and wiggled his hands next to his ears. "Can't catch me!"

The other two goblins on the balcony started laughing smugly, too.

"Not so great now without your fairy magic, are you?" one of them sneered at the girls.

"We have the magic horseshoe, and we're not giving it back!" the other one jeered.

But Rachel had spotted something in the wall of the booth. "Look at this air vent," she said, pointing. "The holes are big enough for a fairy to get through."

"You're right. Follow me," Paige called as she flew through the air vent into the booth. Rachel and Kirsty did the same. Once inside the booth, Paige sent a stream of sparkles over to Kirsty and Rachel, making them human-size again!

The goblin inside the booth was staring out the window, wondering where Paige and the girls had gone. A look of horror crossed his face when he turned and saw the girls inside the booth with him.

"Go away!" he yelled, hugging the horseshoe tightly. "You can't have it! Help!" he called, backing away from the girls.

The two goblins outside dashed to the booth's door and began rattling the handle. But they couldn't get in.

"Give us the horseshoe, please," said Kirsty as she and Rachel moved toward the goblin.

The goblin shook his head furiously. He had backed right up against the counter that controlled the lights. As the girls came closer, he jumped up onto the counter and glared at them.

Rachel tried to grab the horseshoe, but the goblin danced out of her reach. As he did, his big green feet pressed a few of the light switches.

"Hey! What's going on up there?" a loud voice demanded.

"That's Mr. Robinson!" Rachel gasped. She turned to look out the window. Some of the lights on the stage were flashing on and off! The director was staring up at the balcony, and he didn't look happy.

"We have to hurry and get the horseshoe back," Rachel told Kirsty, "before Mr. Robinson sends someone up here to check the lights!"

Perfect Ponies

The goblins on the balcony were still trying to push their way in. But now the goblin inside the booth was determined to get *out*! He jumped down from the control panel, darted past Rachel and Kirsty, and dragged the chair away from the door.

Immediately, the door burst open

and the two goblins tumbled in. They
bumped right into their startled friend.
The horseshoe was knocked out of his
hand, and it flew across the booth!
As the goblins crashed to the floor in
a tangled heap, the magic horseshoe
landed right at Kirsty's feet.

"Thank you!" Kirsty smiled, picking
it up.

Paige fluttered over to the door.
Rachel and Kirsty followed, laughing as
they stepped over the pile of groaning
goblins.

"You'd better hurry up and go,"
Rachel said to the goblins.

"Or we'll put makeup and dresses on
you, and make you part of the play!"
Kirsty added with a grin.

The goblins scowled. Muttering and moaning, they picked themselves up as the girls left the booth.

Kirsty and Rachel hurried down the balcony stairs with Paige flying alongside them. "Thank you so much, girls!" Paige cried as they reached the lobby. "Now I need to go back to Fairyland right away and tell everyone that the magic horseshoe is safe!" She smiled at Rachel and Kirsty. "I'll ask India the Moonstone Fairy to send you sweet dreams so that you sleep well tonight, girls. After all, tomorrow is your big performance! Good-bye!" And with a kiss and a wave, Paige disappeared in a shower of fairy magic.

Rachel and Kirsty hurried back into the auditorium and down the aisle toward the stage. Most of the cast and crew were gathered there together.

"We've looked everywhere," the woman playing Cinderella was saying, "and we can't find the horseshoe."

"Mr. Robinson!" Kirsty called,

walking up to the stage. "Rachel and
I found it!" She held up the glittering
horseshoe.

Alison rushed forward, looking very
relieved. "Thank you, girls," she said
gratefully, taking the horseshoe from
them.

Mr. Robinson clapped his hands.

"Wonderful! Now we can get back to work. Let's start at the pumpkin coach scene."

Rachel and Kirsty hurried into the wings to watch as the rehearsal began again. This time, the ponies performed perfectly. They

waited patiently as Cinderella, wearing a beautiful ball gown and glass slippers, climbed into the coach. Then, at a signal from the Fairy Godmother, they trotted off into the wings. A stagehand

was waiting there to grab their lead
ropes.

"Nice job!" Rachel exclaimed, as she
and Kirsty gave the ponies a pat.

"The horseshoe's magic is making sure
all the props work and no scenery falls
over!" Kirsty whispered happily. "Now
I just have to make sure that *I* don't fall
over when we rehearse our dance."

"You'll be great," Rachel said, putting an arm around Kirsty's shoulder. "We'll do whatever we can to keep the goblins from causing any more trouble before the performance tomorrow night!"

The Show Must Go On

Contents

A Christmas Surprise

"I'm nervous!" Kirsty declared as she and Rachel joined the rest of the cast backstage. "I can't believe the show is tonight. Two days ago, I wasn't even *in* it!"

"No one would guess that," Rachel said. "You didn't make a single mistake in the dress rehearsal yesterday!"

It was Christmas Eve, and the cast of *Cinderella* had gathered backstage before the show.

"Well, this is it, everyone," Mr. Robinson said. "Yesterday's rehearsal was fantastic, and I'm sure you'll be even better tonight with the audience cheering you on!"

Everyone clapped.

"We want the Christmas play to be fun and festive," Mr. Robinson went on. "So don't be afraid to improvise in little ways! And now, here's something to get you all into the Christmas spirit. . . ."

A stagehand stepped forward holding a box full of Christmas crackers! Rachel recognized them right away because her

aunt in England sent her one every year.
They looked like big, wrapped candies,
but if you pulled both ends, they made
a snapping noise! There were fun little
prizes inside, too. Everyone gathered
around to take one.

"It's too bad my
mom and dad
couldn't get tickets
to the play," said
Rachel, selecting a
silver cracker.
Kirsty took a gold one
and nodded in agreement.

"Good luck, everyone!" called Mr.
Robinson, as they hurried off to their
dressing rooms.

As soon as the girls had closed the
door to their dressing room, Rachel held

out her cracker. "Let's see what's inside," she said with a grin.

Kirsty took the other end and pulled. The cracker snapped open with a bang, and a pretty pearl bracelet fell out.

"Now mine," Kirsty said, holding out her cracker.

As Rachel tugged the other end, the cracker snapped open with a burst of golden sparkles. Paige zoomed out from inside! "It's me again, girls!" she announced.

"Jack Frost is determined to ruin the play tonight, so the goblins will be looking for the most powerful magic shoe—Cinderella's glass slipper!"

"That one makes sure that everyone remembers their lines, right?" asked Kirsty.

Paige nodded. "Think how awful it would be if nobody could remember what to say!" she replied. "We have to make sure that Jack Frost and his goblins don't get their hands on that glass slipper!"

All the Wrong Lines

"Let's go check on the glass slippers before we change into our costumes," Rachel suggested.

Paige hid in Rachel's pocket as the girls ran to the props area. Cinderella's ball gown was hanging there, and on the floor below it was a shoe box. Kirsty lifted the lid. She, Rachel, and Paige all

sighed with relief as they saw both glass
slippers nestled inside.

"Can you tell which one is magic?"
Paige asked.

Kirsty looked
closely at the shoes
and noticed that
one gleamed with
a rainbow-colored
shimmer. She pointed
to it.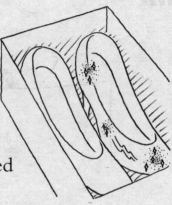

"Yes, that's the magic one," Paige
confirmed, nodding. "Please keep a close
eye on it, girls."

"The stagehands will put the dress and
the shoes in the wings before the show
starts," Rachel explained as they hurried
back to the dressing room. "Luckily,
Kirsty and I enter from the same side

of the stage for our dance."

"So we'll wait there and keep an eye on the shoes the whole time," Kirsty promised.

"I haven't seen any goblins so far," Paige said as she helped Kirsty and Rachel into their costumes.

Rachel jumped as a bell sounded overhead. "That means it's only fifteen minutes to showtime!"

"We'd better get our makeup done," said Kirsty, looking nervous.

"I'll meet you in the wings!" Paige smiled at them. "Good luck. I know you're both going to be great!"

Ten minutes later, Kirsty and Rachel were ready. As they hurried to the wings, they could hear a loud buzz of anticipation coming from the audience on the other side of the curtain.

"There are the glass slippers," Kirsty said, pointing. They had been placed neatly in the wings.

"Hello, girls," Paige whispered, fluttering over to join them. "I've been guarding the slippers, and I haven't seen a single goblin!" "We're just in time," Rachel said as the opening music sounded. "The play is about to start."

She and Kirsty watched as the ugly stepsisters pranced on stage. Their outrageous costumes made the audience roar with laughter! The girls glanced at each other in delight. The play was off to a great start.

As it got closer to the time for the glass slippers to make an appearance, the girls began to feel nervous.

"They go out after the pumpkin coach and the ball gown," Rachel whispered to Kirsty.

Back on stage, the ugly stepsisters had

left for the palace, and Cinderella was all alone. "I wish I could go to the ball!" She sighed.

At just that moment, the Fairy Godmother glided onto the stage. She wore a sparkling silver dress and a wig of golden curls with a silver tiara on top. "I am your Fairy Godmother, and you will go to the ball!" she declared, raising her wand. "You will wear beautiful glass slippers to dance the night away," she added, turning to the wings. "Bring me the glass slippers!" Rachel and Kirsty looked at each other, confused.

"I thought the pumpkin coach was first," Kirsty murmured to Rachel. Cinderella also looked bewildered. "Not the shoes!" she whispered. "The pumpkin!"

The Fairy Godmother scowled. "Fine," she said sulkily. "Bring me a pumpkin!"

Cinderella did. The girls watched as one of the crew members set off a smoke machine so the pumpkin could be removed from the stage. While the stage was covered in smoke, the ponies trotted on pulling the beautiful pumpkin coach. There was a huge burst of applause from the audience.

"Now for the glass slippers!" cried the Fairy Godmother, before the audience had even finished clapping.

Rachel and Kirsty could see that Cinderella was getting annoyed.

"No, the ball gown!" they heard her whisper.

"This is weird," Rachel said. "Alison never gets her lines wrong."

"Well, the goblins don't have the magic slipper," Paige said, pointing at the glass shoes waiting in the wings. "So that isn't why Alison's forgetting her lines!"

"Her voice sounds a little funny," Kirsty added. "Maybe she's getting a cold."

"And now for your ball gown, Cinderella!" shouted the Fairy Godmother. There was another puff of smoke and a stagehand helped Cinderella put on the dress. A gasp of delight rose from the audience as the smoke cleared and they saw the sparkling ball gown for the first time.

"And *now* for the glass slippers!" the Fairy Godmother said loudly, walking closer to the wings where Kirsty and Rachel stood.

Kirsty peered at the Fairy Godmother. Something strange seemed to be hanging from her chin. When Kirsty looked more closely, she saw that it was an icicle!

"Rachel!" Kirsty whispered. "That's not the Fairy Godmother—it's Jack Frost!"

Flying Shoes

"It can't be!" Rachel exclaimed.

"It is!" Paige gasped, staring at Jack Frost. "But how did he make himself as tall as Alison, who's supposed to be playing the Fairy Godmother?"

Paige and the girls knew that there was a special rule in Fairyland. It kept anyone from using magic to make themselves taller than the highest tower of the Fairyland palace. But the girls didn't have time to think about that

now. Jack Frost was waving the Fairy Godmother's wand, eyes gleaming as he looked at the glass slippers in the wings. When the stagehand set off the smoke machine, Jack Frost reached eagerly for the slippers. As the Fairy Godmother, he was supposed to hand them to Cinderella, but Rachel

and Kirsty knew that he would just run
off with them.

"Oh, no you don't!" Kirsty murmured,
snatching the glass slippers out of Jack
Frost's reach.

"Give me those IMMEDIATELY!"
Jack Frost roared.

The audience began to chuckle,
thinking that it was all part of the show.
As smoke filled the stage, Jack Frost
leaned over and tried to grab the slippers

from Kirsty. She quickly
handed them to Rachel,
who backed away from
Jack Frost's icy fingers.
"What do we do now?"
asked Rachel, clutching
the slippers.

The smoke cleared
again and the audience
laughed loudly as Jack
Frost jumped up and down with rage on
the stage. "GIVE ME THOSE GLASS
SLIPPERS!" he howled.

"We have to get the slippers to

Cinderella somehow, or we'll ruin the show!" Kirsty said urgently. "But how can we make sure Cinderella gets them, and not Jack Frost?"

"Like this," Paige whispered. As the stagehand turned on the smoke machine again, Paige waved her wand. A stream of sparkles lifted the glass slippers from Rachel's grasp and carried them across the stage, past Jack Frost and into the arms of a very surprised Cinderella.

The audience clapped and laughed, clearly having a wonderful time. But

Jack Frost just glared at Kirsty and Rachel as Cinderella put on the slippers and climbed into the pumpkin coach.

"Have a good time at the ball!" he snapped coldly to Cinderella. "But be home by midnight—or else!" Then he stomped off into the wings on the other side of the stage.

"Well, the magic glass slipper is safe

so far," Rachel said anxiously, as the ponies pulled the coach offstage. "But I bet Jack Frost will be waiting for another chance to steal it!" She shivered just thinking about it.

If the Shoe Fits . . .

"It's almost time for our dance," Kirsty whispered.

Onstage, Cinderella had arrived at the ball, and was dancing her first romantic waltz with the prince.

"Paige, can you look out for Jack Frost and the goblins while we're performing?" asked Rachel.

Paige nodded. "If I'm up
high, I'll be able to see
everything," she
whispered, zooming
toward the ceiling to hide
among the spotlights.

Karen and Lucy hurried over to join
Rachel and Kirsty in the wings. As
the waltz music finished, the prince led

Cinderella to a golden
chair. She sat down,
arranging her
skirt so that
her glass
slippers were
on display.
"We're on,"

Rachel whispered as the music for their dance began. "Good luck, everybody."

Rachel skipped lightly out of the wings, leading the girls to the center of the stage. Kirsty took her place between Rachel and Karen. She was determined to get the steps right, but she couldn't help wondering what Jack Frost and his goblins were up to!

Concentrate, she told herself.

The music began. And before she
knew it, Kirsty had performed the whole
dance without making a single mistake!
BONG! BONG! BONG!

Right on cue, the clock began to
chime midnight. Kirsty and
Rachel watched as
Cinderella jumped from
her chair. She ran up
the stairs at the back of
the stage, leaving the
magic glass slipper
on the third step.
It glittered
like a diamond
under the bright white
spotlights.

A small child dressed in a furry gray

mouse costume darted over and grabbed the slipper, just as the prince stepped forward to pick it up.

"Who's that? There isn't supposed to be a mouse!" Rachel whispered to Kirsty backstage.

"I bet it's a goblin!" Kirsty gasped. Sure enough, when the girls looked closely, they could see a green face behind the mouse mask!

Meanwhile, the prince was trying to wrestle the slipper from the mouse's grasp. "Hey, I'm supposed to take that!" he muttered as the audience howled with laughter.

After a minute or two, the prince managed to grab the slipper away. He held it up. "I promise I will find the owner of this glass slipper—and marry her!" he declared, as the mouse stormed furiously offstage.

The audience applauded, the curtain came down, and everyone hurried into the wings. The stagehands quickly began to change the scenery, ready for the final scene.

"Thank goodness the prince didn't let that goblin get away with the glass slipper!" Paige whispered, landing on Kirsty's shoulder as the curtain rose again.

The girls watched from the wings as the prince and his servants arrived at Cinderella's house with the glass slipper. The first ugly stepsister tried the shoe on, but it didn't fit. Prince Charming shook his head and moved on to the other sister.

"Why does the second ugly

stepsister look so much meaner than usual?" Rachel asked. Then she clapped a hand over her mouth. "It's Jack Frost!" she exclaimed.

"We have to stop the prince from giving him the magic slipper!" Kirsty said anxiously.

But it was too late. The prince was

down on one knee, trying to fit the slipper onto the ugly stepsister's foot. Rachel and Kirsty could see that the foot was big, green, and knobbly. It was a goblin's foot!

"So *that's* how Jack Frost is making himself so tall," Rachel whispered. "He's standing on a goblin's shoulders!"

The audience thought that the big green foot was a great joke. They roared with laughter, though the prince looked a little confused as he tried the slipper on the goblin's foot. "This slipper doesn't fit," he announced, shaking his head.

"It *does* fit!" Jack Frost snapped. "Give it to me. I'll show you!" He grabbed the slipper from the prince and tried to hurry offstage.

Immediately, the prince blocked his way. "Give that back!" he demanded.

"No way!" Jack Frost sneered. The audience chuckled as Kirsty, Rachel, and Paige watched in dismay from the wings.

"Footmen!" the prince called desperately. "Help me!"

"The prince is calling for his servants," Paige whispered, waving  her wand so that Kirsty and Rachel were suddenly wearing red uniforms with gold buttons. "That's your cue, girls!" she finished.

Rachel and Kirsty ran onto the stage.

"We're here, Your Highness!" Kirsty announced.

The girls and the prince surrounded Jack Frost. He had nowhere to go, so Jack Frost threw the glass slipper sulkily at the prince, who caught it. Grinning at each other, Rachel and Kirsty stepped to the side of the stage as Cinderella arrived to try on the slipper.

"It fits!" the prince announced to loud cheers from the audience. "Will you marry me, Cinderella?"

"I will," Cinderella replied, "and we'll live happily ever after!"

The prince and Cinderella began to walk off into the wings as the audience applauded. But Kirsty noticed that Jack Frost was following them!

Thinking quickly, she stepped forward. "That ugly stepsister won't leave Cinderella alone!" she called to the audience. "Let's all warn Cinderella, okay?"

"Look out behind you, Cinderella!"

153

shouted a little girl in the front row.

Cinderella stopped and looked around. Jack Frost put his hands in his pockets and whistled a tune, trying to look innocent.

Cinderella and the prince walked on, but Jack Frost crept behind them again.

"Look out behind you, Cinderella!" Kirsty and Rachel shouted, and this time, the audience joined in.

Cinderella turned and Jack Frost folded his arms, pretending to study the painted scenery.

Then, just as Cinderella and her prince were about to leave the stage, Rachel saw Jack Frost pull his wand out of his pocket. "Oh, no!" she whispered. "Jack Frost is going to cast a spell!"

A Standing Ovation

Kirsty desperately looked around for inspiration. How could they stop Jack Frost?

Suddenly, she noticed that Jack Frost and the goblin were standing on a trapdoor in the stage. She quickly turned to the wings, looking for Paige. She could see a faint sparkle in the air where

the little fairy was hovering. Trying
to quietly get her attention, Kirsty
pointed at Jack Frost and then down at
the trapdoor. She hoped Paige would
understand!

Jack Frost raised his wand, but just as
he started to say a spell, the trapdoor
opened. Both the goblin and Jack Frost
fell through the hole! The audience
clapped enthusiastically, thinking it was
all part of the play.

"Merry Christmas, everyone!" called the prince and Cinderella together as the whole cast gathered onstage to bow. The applause and cheers were deafening as the audience gave the Christmas play a standing ovation.

Rachel and Kirsty smiled happily at each other. Even though Jack Frost and his goblins had done their best to ruin it, the play had been a huge success.

Once the curtain came down, the

audience began to leave. Meanwhile,
the cast rushed backstage to change.

"Wasn't that fun?"
Rachel cried. "We
didn't let Jack Frost
ruin our play.
In fact, it was
fantastic!"
"The audience loved
it," Kirsty agreed.
"You were wonderful!"
Paige told the girls, fluttering overhead.
"You stopped Jack Frost from stealing
the magic glass slipper, and now
children all over the world can enjoy
their Christmas plays!"

As the girls entered their dressing room,
all the lights around the dressing

table mirror began to flash. A vivid
rainbow appeared, stretching from one
side of the room to the other. As Kirsty
and Rachel watched with wide eyes, the
king and queen of the fairies stepped off
the end of the rainbow.

"Girls, we've come to thank you for what you have done." Queen Titania smiled. "You saved Christmas!"

"And we sent Jack Frost back to Fairyland," King Oberon added. "He won't be causing any more trouble this Christmas."

"What happened to the real Fairy Godmother and ugly stepsister?" Kirsty asked anxiously.

"Jack Frost froze them so he could

take their places," the queen replied.
"But don't worry, we thawed them
out!"

"They won't remember anything," the
king chimed in. "Except that the play
was a huge success."

Just then, there was a knock at the
door.

"We have to
go," said Queen
Titania quickly.
She, Paige, and
the king stepped
onto the end of
the rainbow.

"Merry Christmas,
girls, and thank you!" Paige cried,
blowing kisses to them.

"And there's one more Christmas surprise waiting for you!" the king added as the rainbow whisked them away. "Good-bye. . . ."

Rachel opened the door and couldn't believe her eyes. Her mom and dad were standing outside with Kirsty's parents!

"We saw the show!" Mrs. Walker announced, beaming at Rachel and Kirsty.

"You were both wonderful!" Mrs. Tate said.

"Great job," added Mr. Walker, and Kirsty's dad nodded. All four of them looked very proud!

"But the show was sold out," Kirsty said, looking confused. "How did you get tickets?"

"Well, it was strange," said Mr. Walker with a frown. "We both had Christmas cards pushed under our doors this afternoon. The cards weren't signed, but there were tickets to the play inside them!"

"So we rushed over to Tippington, met up with Rachel's parents, and got here just before the show started!" explained Mr. Tate.

"We'll wait outside while you get changed," Mrs. Tate said. Then she winked. "And bundle up, girls, it's snowing outside!" she added.

Rachel couldn't help giggling as she

shut the door. "Well, I think I know where those tickets came from."

"Yes, from our fairy friends!" Kirsty said with a grin. "And now we can really enjoy Christmas, knowing that Jack Frost and his goblins can't ruin it for everyone. It's going to be a merry Christmas after all!"

SPECIAL EDITION

Don't miss Rachel and Kirsty's
other holiday adventures!

Take a special sneak peek at

Stella
the Star Fairy!

Darkness Falls

Mrs. Tate popped her head around
the door. "Are you ready, girls?"
she asked. "It's time to leave for the
Christmas Fair."

"Coming, Mom," Kirsty said,
jumping up.

"I'm really glad I could come and

visit," said Rachel Walker, as she followed her best friend into the hall to get their coats. Rachel was visiting over Christmas break. Her parents were picking her up on Christmas Eve.

"Me, too," Kirsty replied. "You're going to love the fair. And who knows . . . we might even see a Christmas fairy!"

Rachel and Kirsty thought they were the luckiest girls in the world, because they had become friends with the fairies! Whenever the fairies were in trouble, they asked the girls for help. Usually cold Jack Frost was causing magical mayhem with the help of his nasty goblins.

"I forgot to tell you!" Kirsty said, pulling on her boots. "Every year, someone from my school is chosen to be the fair's Christmas King or Queen. This year, it's my friend Molly."

"Wow! I bet she's really excited," said Rachel, smiling. "I'd love to be the Christmas Queen!"

Kirsty nodded as her parents joined them.

"Everybody ready?" Mrs. Tate said. "Then let's go!"

"Did someone turn off the Christmas tree lights?" Mr. Tate asked. "They were on a few minutes ago, but now they're not."

Everyone shook their heads. Kirsty peeked into the living room, where the tree stood. "The switch is still on," she pointed out.

"The lights must be broken," Mr. Tate

decided. "Never mind, I'll fix them when we get back."

"Yes, it's time to go," Kirsty's mom agreed. "The parade starts soon!"

Quickly, they all left the house and walked up Twisty Lane toward High Street and Wetherbury Market Square.

"I can hear music," Rachel said, clapping her hands excitedly.

Even though it was a cold, frosty night, the square was packed with people! They bustled around stalls selling brightly-painted tree decorations, Christmas cookies, hot chocolate, and gifts. There was even a merry tune playing on an old organ.

"Isn't it great?" Kirsty said, her eyes shining. She pointed at a raised platform in the middle of the square. The mayor

of Wetherbury was standing there next to
a large switch. "It'll be even better when
the Christmas Queen turns on the lights,"
Kirsty added.

Rachel glanced around. She could see
dark shapes made out of unlit lightbulbs
above their heads, but it was hard to
figure out what the shapes were. She
was looking forward to seeing them all
lit up.

"Ooh, I can't wait to see Molly!"
Kirsty exclaimed, as the parade began.

The first float that rumbled into the
square was decorated like Santa's
workshop. Elves were making toys, and
Santa sat on a golden sleigh!

"Oh, look!" Rachel gasped, as another
float came into view. It carried a huge
dollop of papier-mâché fruitcake with

a sprig of holly on top. More floats followed, all looking colorful and Christmassy!

"Here's Molly," Kirsty said to Rachel as the final float appeared. "Doesn't she look pretty?"

Kirsty's friend was dressed in white and silver. Her dress had a long full skirt, scattered here and there with sparkling snowflakes. She wore a glittering silver tiara on her head and sat on a jeweled throne, waving at the crowd. Behind her was an ice palace, decorated with gleaming icicles.

Rachel nudged Kirsty. "The Christmas Queen's palace is much prettier than Jack Frost's gloomy ice castle!" she whispered. Kirsty nodded eagerly.

The float stopped next to the platform. The mayor helped Molly up the steps as the crowd clapped.

"I would like to wish everyone in Wetherbury a very merry Christmas!" Molly announced. Then she pulled the light switch with a flourish.

The square lit up in a blaze of color as the lightbulbs sprang to life. Everyone *ooh*ed and *aah*ed as they gazed around.

"This is amazing!" Kirsty breathed.

"It's beautiful," Rachel agreed.

There were hundreds of snowflakes in different sizes strung on wires overhead, and they all glittered with rainbow-colored lights.

The Christmas Queen had come down from the platform now and was waving at the two girls.

"Hi, there!" Molly called, her face glowing with excitement. "Did you like my float?"

"It was beautiful!" Kirsty replied. "Molly, this is my friend Rachel."

"Hi, Molly," said Rachel, admiring Molly's sparkling dress. "You look so pretty!"

"And these are definitely the best lights Wetherbury has ever had!" Kirsty added.

But just then, one of the snowflakes above their heads began to flicker. As the girls glanced upward, every single one of the beautiful snowflake lights suddenly went out!

RAINBOW magic™
THE RAINBOW FAIRIES

Find the magic in every book!

www.scholastic.com
www.rainbowmagiconline.com

HiT entertainment

RAINBOW

RAINBOW magic

THE JEWEL FAIRIES

They Make Fairyland Sparkle!

India the Moonstone Fairy by Daisy Meadows

Scarlett the Garnet Fairy by Daisy Meadows

Emily the Emerald Fairy by Daisy Meadows

Chloe the Topaz Fairy by Daisy Meadows

Amy the Amethyst Fairy by Daisy Meadows

Sophie the Sapphire Fairy by Daisy Meadows

Lucy the Diamond Fairy by Daisy Meadows

RAINBOW magic™

THE PETAL FAIRIES

Keep Fairyland in Bloom!

SCHOLASTIC

www.scholastic.com

www.rainbowmagiconline.com

HiT entertainment

PFAIRIES

RAINBOW magic™

There's Magic in Every Series!

The Rainbow Fairies

The Weather Fairies

The Jewel Fairies

The Pet Fairies

The Fun Day Fairies

The Petal Fairies

The Dance Fairies

The Music Fairies

The Sports Fairies

The Party Fairies

The Ocean Fairies

Read them all!

■ SCHOLASTIC

HiT entertainment

www.scholastic.com

www.rainbowmagiconline.com

RMFAIRY3